WEDDING
M U S I C

©Copyright 1987 Benson Publications. All rights controlled by
The Zondervan Music Group, Nashville.

THE FOLLOWING WEDDING ACCOMPANIMENT CASSETTES ARE AVAILABLE FROM THE BENSON COMPANY:

WT20001	THE BRIDAL CHORUS/THE WEDDING MARCH - fully orchestrated cassette for use as procession music.
WT20023	PRELUDE MUSIC - fully orchestrated cassette for use as an instrumental prelude to the service. Contains the following songs: Jesu, Joy Of Man's Desiring/Sheep May Safely Graze/Air For G String
WT20024	POSTLUDE MUSIC - fully orchestrated cassette for use as an instrumental postlude to the service. Contains the following songs: Excerpts from Handel's Water Music/ Canon by Pachelbel/Ode To Joy (Beethoven's Ninth Symphony)
WT20012	TRUMPET VOLUNTARY - contains a listening demonstration and a performance accompaniment cassette. (Instrumental)
WT20000	SAMPLER CASSETTE - contains a listening demonstration to each of the songs listed below:

(The following cassettes contain both a high voice and a low voice background accompaniment track for use by a soloist and a listening demonstration with a pre-recorded soloist's voice.)

WT20010	ETERNAL LIFE (THE PRAYER OF ST. FRANCIS)
WT20020	EVERGREEN
WT20005	HOUSEHOLD OF FAITH
WT20009	I'VE WAITED A LIFETIME
WT20022	LONGER
WT20008	LORD'S PRAYER, THE
WT20006	MORNING HAS BROKEN
WT20003	NATURE OF LOVE
WT20016	NOBODY LOVES ME LIKE YOU DO
WT20002	ONLY GOD COULD LOVE YOU MORE
WT20013	OUR SACRED PLEDGE
WT20004	SAVIOR, LIKE A SHEPHERD LEAD US
WT20021	THAT'S WHAT FRIENDS ARE FOR
WT20007	THERE IS LOVE (A WEDDING SONG)
WT20017	UP WHERE WE BELONG
WT20018	WE'VE ONLY JUST BEGUN
WT20014	WHAT A DIFFERENCE YOU'VE MADE IN MY LIFE
WT20011	WIND BENEATH MY WINGS
WT20015	YOU DECORATED MY LIFE
WT20019	YOU'RE THE INSPIRATION

MT10063   AFTER ALL THOSE YEARS - as recorded by Farrell & Farrell is also very appropriate for wedding use. (Available through the Benson MASTERTRAX series.)

INDEX

1. Because 38
2. Bridal Chorus, The 8
3. Entreat Me Not To Leave Thee 86
4. Eternal Life (The Prayer of St. Francis) 46
5. Father Says, "I Do", The 96
6. Hearts Of Joy 61
7. Household Of Faith 67
8. I've Waited A Lifetime 41
9. Jesu, Joy Of Man's Desiring 63
10. Make Us One 82
11. Morning Has Broken 55
12. Nature Of Love 99
13. Only God Could Love You More 74
14. Our Sacred Pledge 23
15. Savior, Like A Shepherd Lead Us 91
16. There Is Love (A Wedding Song) 15
17. This Is Where The Candle Glows 52
18. Trumpet Voluntary 71
19. We Are One 34
20. Wedding March, The 103
21. What A Difference You've Made In My Life 29
22. Wind Beneath My Wings 77
23. You Decorated My Life 26

TOPICAL INDEX

Statement of Purpose

Hearts of Joy
Our Sacred Pledge
There Is Love
Nature of Love
Savior, Like a Shepherd Lead Us

The Giving of the Bride

The Father Says, "I Do"
Morning Has Broken
Wind Beneath My Wings

Exhortation to the Bride and Groom

I've Waited a Lifetime
Nature of Love

The Marriage Vows

Only God Could Love You More
Our Sacred Pledge
Make Us One
* You're the Inspiration
* Nobody Loves Me Like You Do

Reading of Scripture

Because
Eternal Life (The Prayer of St. Francis)
* The Lord's Prayer

Exchange of Rings

Entreat Me Not to Leave Thee
Household of Faith
I've Waited a Lifetime
Savior, Like a Shepherd Lead Us
What a Difference You've Made in My Life
You Decorated My Life
* Evergreen
* You're the Inspiration
* That's What Friends Are For
* Longer
* Nobody Loves Me Like You Do

Lighting the Unity Candle

This Is Where the Candle Glows
We Are One
* Evergreen
* That's What Friends Are For
* Longer

Prayer for the Bride and Groom

Household of Faith
Make Us One
Savior, Like a Shepherd Lead Us
* The Lord's Prayer
* Up Where We Belong

The Pronouncement of Marriage

The Father Says, "I Do"
* Evergreen
* We've Only Just Begun

Benediction

Eternal Life
Savior, Like a Shepherd Lead Us
* The Lord's Prayer
* Up Where We Belong

Presentation of the Newlyweds

* We've Only Just Begun
* That's What Friends Are For

Processional, Recessional, Prelude and Postlude

The Bridal Chorus
The Wedding March
Jesu, Joy of Man's Desiring
Trumpet Voluntary
* Prelude Music
* Postlude Music

*These songs are available as Wedding Accompaniment Cassettes from The Benson Company, but are not included in this book. Many of your favorites from this book are also available in accompaniment cassette form. A full listing may be found on page 2.

PRE - WEDDING PLANNER

3 Months Before Wedding

* BOOK THE CHURCH
* FIND A PASTOR
* BOOK RECEPTION HALL
* FIND A CATERER
* FIND A FLORIST
* FIND PHOTOGRAPHER/VIDEO CAMERAMAN
* ORDER INVITATIONS
* ORDER BRIDESMAIDS' DRESSES
* ORDER BRIDE'S DRESS
* GET INVITATION LIST TOGETHER
* MAKE HONEYMOON RESERVATIONS
* FIND A PIANIST/ORGANIST
* FIND A SOLOIST/SINGER
* REGISTER FOR GIFTS
* COORDINATE MOTHERS' DRESSES
* SHOP FOR TROUSSEAU

2 Months Before Wedding

* GET BLACK AND WHITE PICTURE MADE FOR ENGAGEMENT ANNOUNCEMENT
* ADDRESS INVITATIONS
* CHOOSE WEDDING RINGS
* MAKE HOTEL RESERVATIONS FOR OUT-OF-TOWN GUESTS
* CHOOSE FOOD FOR REHEARSAL DINNER
* SELECT THE MUSIC
* PURCHASE ACCESSORIES (Toasting Glasses, Flower Baskets, etc.)
* PLAN ATTENDANTS' PARTY

1 Month Before Wedding

* CHOOSE TUXEDOS
* MAIL INVITATIONS 4-6 WEEKS BEFORE
* BUY BRIDESMAIDS AND GROOMSMEN GIFTS
* GET MARRIAGE LICENSE
* FINAL FITTING FOR WEDDING DRESS
* BUY SHOES, VEIL, HOSE, GARTER, SLIP
* HAVE WEDDING PORTRAIT MADE
* PUT ENGAGEMENT ANNOUNCEMENT IN LOCAL PAPER
* MEET WITH PASTOR ABOUT SERVICE
* MEET WITH WEDDING DIRECTOR
* MEET WITH FLORIST AND CATERER
* CHANGE NAME ON CREDIT CARDS, CHECKS, ETC.
* BUY GIFT FOR FIANCE
* BUY GOING AWAY OUTFIT
* MAIL WEDDING ANNOUNCEMENT TO PAPER
* CONFIRM HONEYMOON ARRANGEMENTS AND PICK UP TICKETS AND TRAVELER'S CHECKS

WEDDING SERVICE PLANNER

It seems rather presumptious to actually print what is to be a "contemporary" wedding ceremony. Tastes differ even within a local church and when you consider an entire country in which freedom of expression is so highly cherished, it seems almost ridiculous to print one ceremony and call it "the one". Nonetheless, we believe that this printed ceremony can be valuable to you in at least two ways. First of all, it will provide you with a written example. Examples are especially useful because you can either use them as they are or change them to your liking. Secondly, this example will reflect some things that have come to be seen as traditional. Traditions are helpful to us in that they have developed time-honored meanings; they help us to reach a common understanding of what a wedding means. The following wedding service will hopefully be seen as a helpful example; something that you can change to your taste, yet still have enough tradition to know what it is for! Here is the outline of this ceremony:

PROCESSIONAL - (Get Everyone Into The Church.)
INVOCATION - (The Pastor States Why Everyone Is Here And Welcomes Them.)
THE BRIDE IS GIVEN AWAY - (Two Families Give Up Part Of Themselves To Form A New Family.)
CHARGES TO THE BRIDE AND GROOM - (The Couple Publicly States Why They Are Here.)
VOWS - (Public Promises Of Commitment.)
RINGS - (Symbolic Gifts.)
PRONOUNCEMENT - (The Marriage Is Officially Declared.)
PRAYER - (Blessings On The Couple.)
ANNOUNCEMENT - (Now Everybody Knows!)
RECESSIONAL - (Get Everyone Out Of The Church.)

We hope that this is a helpful tool for your wedding. Consult with the officiating person for further help in planning the ceremony. Professional wedding consultants are available in many places. AND finally, the answer to the question you never think about until you get married... *The Bride Stands On The Groom's Left!*

THE CEREMONY

PRELUDE - (Music for the seating of guests. Use the "prelude" music or even a collection of some of the other songs in this book.)

PROCESSIONAL - (The "Bridal Chorus" is traditionally used, but you may want to use anything else that you see as a theme song for the bride. How about "Jesu, Joy Of Man's Desiring" or "Trumpet Voluntary"? Everyone usually stands as the bride enters.)

INVOCATION - (Everyone still standing.) <u>Pastor Prays:</u> Eternal Father, bless us with an awareness of Your presence as we worship and celebrate (today/tonight). We praise You for creating us in love, and making our hearts restless until we respond in love to You, and to each other. Bless (Groom) and (Bride) who stand here now. We ask Your divine blessing on them in this high moment of their lives. Make them mindful of Your helpfulness in the past and give them confidence that You will continue to help them be true to the vows they will make to each other before You here (today/tonight). In Christ's name, AMEN.

<u>Pastor</u> (To the guests, who are now seated.): Man has alway felt a need to celebrate the great moments of life. Friends and loved ones, (Groom) and (Bride) have invited you here today to witness this great moment in their lives; their wedding today is an occasion for all of you to celebrate in this joyous service of worship, in which these two give themselves to each other and to God. You are here at this wedding (today/tonight) because you are an important part of (Groom) and (Bride)'s lives. You have touched them in the past and now they will look to you to stand with them in the years to come and help strengthen their bonds in times of struggle. Marriage is a union used in scripture to show the relationship between Christ and the Church. It is a relationship of giving. With this in mind, we ask,

"Who gives this woman to be married to this man?"

<u>Father of the bride</u> (or his representative): "I Do." (or, "Her mother and I.")

SONG - "There Is Love (A Wedding Song)" or "Our Sacred Pledge" would work well here.

<u>Pastor</u> (To the bride and groom): (Groom) and (Bride), God has ordained marriage as a covenant between two persons who are in a covenant with Him, so it is God who is joining you together. He will seal your covenant with the eternal dimensions of His covenant, so that you can be an instrument of His will and purpose. You have joyously responded to God's gift of love. Now He will create out of your love something that has never existed before: a holy union in marriage.

God's covenant with man is a covenant of love which offers privileges and responsibilities. Thus, you must make this moment one of the highest spiritual moments of your life - a time of commitment to God and to each other. Because of the strength of the covenant, it alters all other relationships. "For this cause shall a man leave his father and mother and shall cleave to his wife and the two shall become one."

Being in love is the most selfless of experiences, for we are taken out of ourselves and are concerned with another. Love is a way of living, and is sacrificial - not a self-conscious martyrdom, but the discovery of another life which is as dear as one's own. To love is to recognize in another the nature and purpose of one's own existence. Love is selfless service - it seeks always to create happiness, to build confidence, to insure a sense of selfworth and fulfillment. All for the good of the one loved. Love is continuous. It is never interrupted while one decided whether or not it is deserved. Love is patient; it never grows weary when results are not evident. Love is endless; it is never suspended as a threat of ultimate withdrawal. One who loves is always confident, but never arrogant, secure in the certainty that love is of God.

Marriage demands the giving of all that one is - *without reserve* to another... The commitment of the couple to each other, their shared values and goals, is a costly devotion of one's whole being to another who has been carefully chosen; the opening up of inner lives to each other without deceit or defense. When we love somebody, we trust them fully, we expect nothing but good things from them even if appearances are against them. Marriage then becomes a miracle: In one's relationship with another, through one flesh as part of God's process and design, one is re-created in another.

In Christian marriage there are vows to be lived by. A promise will be made in the covenant and it must be kept. "Fidelity is the mark of marriage - not love, not romance, not harmony, not peace - but fidelity and promise." You have heard these words of admonition and instruction concerning the place of marriage in God's covenant. Do you now consent together to be faithful in the obligations of this sacred relationship in all its dimensions? Do you each promise before God and in the presence of this group of friends and witnesses to receive each other as husband and wife, pledging yourselves to love each other and to make every reasonable exertion to promote each other's welfare until the union into which you are now entering is dissolved by death? Do you promise to join with the other in making a home that shall endure in love and peace? Do you realize that the following declarations are unequivocal because they contain no conditional clauses and are declared in God's presence?

VOWS - (Pastor continues) Would you please join hands. (Couple joins hands, still facing pastor.)

I ask of you, (Groom), will you take this woman to be your wife? Will you do everything in your power to make your love for her a growing part of your being? Will you continue to strengthen it from day to day from the best resources of your life? Will you stand by her in health and sickness, in plenty or want, in success or failure, in duty and service, at home or abroad, according to the ordinances of God? (<u>Groom</u>: "I Will.")

I ask of you, (Bride), will you take this man to be your husband? Will you do everything in your power to make your love for him a growing part of your being? Will you continue to strengthen it from day to day from the best resources of your life? Will you stand with him in health and sickness, in plenty or want, in success or failure, in duty and service, at home or abroad, according to the ordinances of God? (<u>Bride</u>: "I Will.")

(Groom and Bride turn to face each other)

Pastor: Repeat after me. (First Groom, Then Bride)
I chose you alone / from all the world / to love and cherish / throughout all the changes of life. / I dedicate myself to you alone / and to your life's work / to join with you / so that together / we may serve God and others / as long as we live. / God be my help.

RINGS - (Pastor continues) Wedding rings serve as an outward and visible sign of an inward and invisible love which binds hearts together. As they are of the finest of earth's materials, so love is the richest of spiritual values. As rings are without edge or seam, having no beginning and no ending, so they symbolize the perfection of a love that cannot end.

(Minister gets rings from best man and maid of honor.)
(Repeat these statements after the minister, or if you are able and want to say them to each other, memorize them. You could do the same with the vows.)

This ring I give you / as an emblem of the covenant made between us this day / and as a pledge of our mutual love. / May it ever be a witness / to all of the inward and spiritual bond of our love / in the name of the Father, Son, and Holy Spirit.

SONG - (See Unity Candle)

(This is a good place for the lighting of the Unity Candle. This is becoming a common tradition, but is still an effective ceremony because it is so visual and because it offers a chance to incorporate your parents if you desire. The basic idea is that two smaller candles are lit before the service and at this point the bride and groom each take a lighted candle and together light a larger, center candle and blow out their individual candles. This symbolizes their new unity. Variations include: 1. Having the parents light the two individual candles before the service; 2. Giving the extinguished candles back to the parents, perhaps with a rose; 3. Doing the whole candle ceremony during a song, such as "Our Sacred Pledge", "Only God Could Love You More", or "This Is Where The Candle Glows".)

(If the candle ceremony is used, the pastor can say this immediately after the vows):

PASTOR - You will no longer be two, but one. During the years of your youth, you lived individual lives. You thought, planned, and acted as individuals. These two lit candles are the same way, two distinct separate lights, each capable of going its separate way. But now your thoughts are for each other, not just for yourself. When you light the center candle together and extinguish your own, it will represent the union of your lives into one. Just as one light cannot be divided, so will your one light be a testimony of your unity in the Lord Jesus Christ.

PRONOUNCEMENT - (Pastor says to bride and groom, after the song) Because you two have desired to be one in Christian marriage and have proclaimed this before God, affirming your acceptance of the responsibilites of such a union and pledging your faith and love to each other, sealing your vows in the giving and receiving of rings, <u>you are husband and wife in the sight of God.</u> Let all people here and everywhere recognize and respect this holy union now and forever. Sir, you may kiss the bride.

PRAYER/BLESSING - Let us pray: Eternal God, we praise You for creating mankind male and female, so that each may find fulfillment in the other. We praise You for all the ways in which Your love comes into our lives, and for all the joys that can come to men and women through marriage. We now commend to Your care and keeping these whom You have here joined together. In times of joy, happiness, sorrow or affliction, may they not demand of You a reason for everything, but may they walk confident of their covenant with You. Help them to realize that You teach us in many ways. AMEN.

ANNOUNCEMENT - Pastor: (to the guests)
It is my priviledge and joy to present to you Mr. and Mrs. _____ .

(At this point, the Recessional music begins. "The Wedding March" is traditional. Other possibilities include: "We've Only Just Begun", "Trumpet Voluntary", or "You're The Inspiration" -- something that celebrates!

RECESSIONAL - (Music for the guests while they're waiting to greet you in the reception line)

* For a shorter Processional, proceed directly to the final six measures.

There Is Love
(A Wedding Song)

N. P. S.

NOEL PAUL STOOKEY

© Copyright 1971 by Public Domain Foundation, Inc. International copyright secured. All rights reserved. Used by permission.

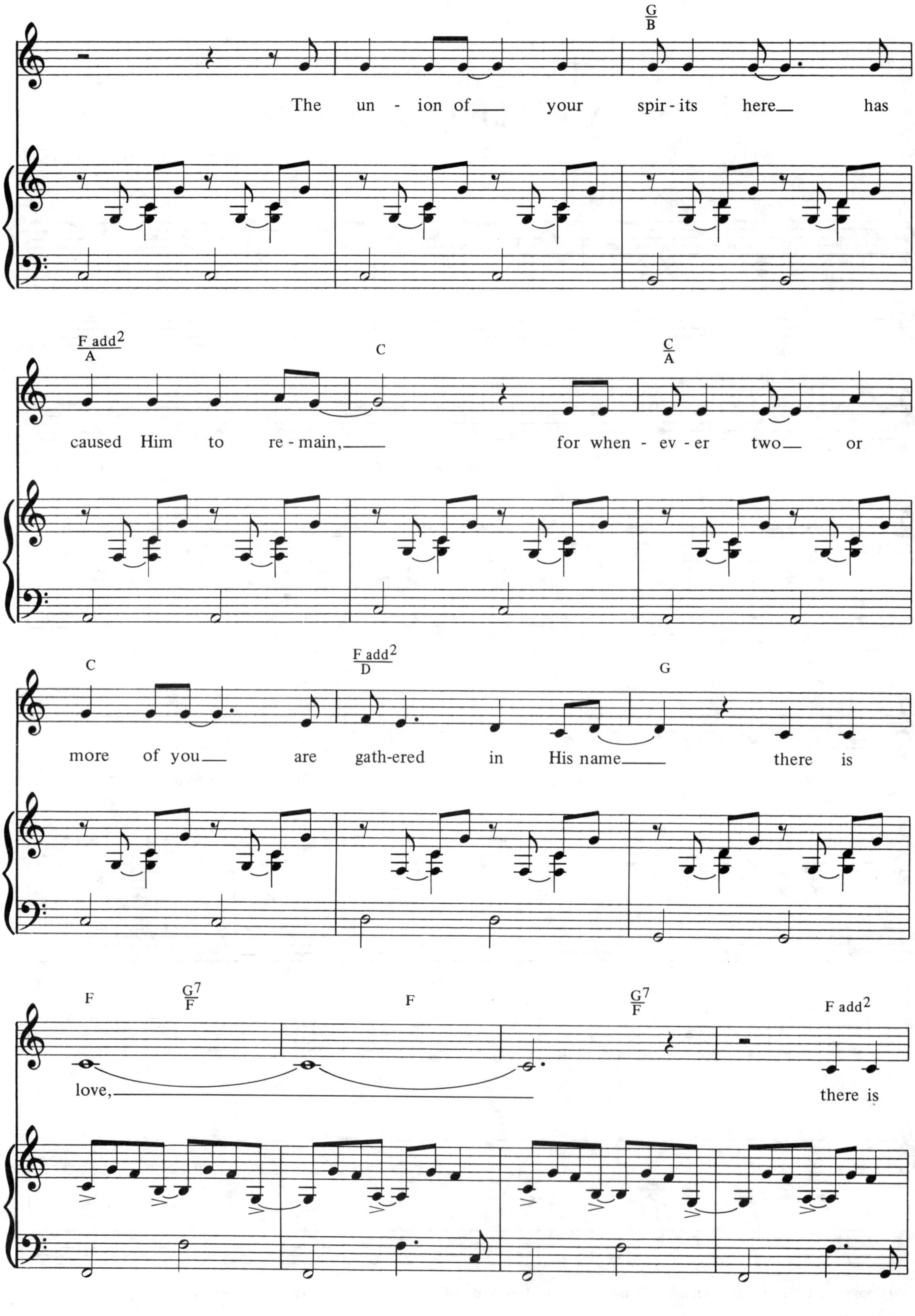
G/B
The union of your spirits here has
F add2/A
C
C/A
caused Him to re-main, for when-ev-er two or
C
F add2/D
G
more of you are gath-ered in His name there is
F
G7/F
F
G7/F
F add2
love, there is

Our Sacred Pledge

Words and Music by
PAT TERRY

© Copyright 1986 by Paragon Music Corp./ASCAP and Pat Terry Music/ASCAP. All rights reserved.
International copyright secured. Used by permission.

You Decorated My Life

Words and Music by
BOB MORRISON and DEBBIE HUPP

Copyright © 1978 by Music City Music, Inc., Nashville, Tennessee. All rights reserved. Used by permission.

What a Difference You've Made in My Life!

A. J.   ARCHIE JORDAN

Copyright © 1977 by Jack and Bill Music Company (c/o The Welk Music Group, Santa Monica, CA 90401). International copyright secured. All rights reserved. Used by permission.

We Are One

Words and Music by
CHUCK BENTLEY and MARK GERSMEHL

© Copyright 1984 by Paragon Music Corp./ASCAP and LifeSong Music Press/BMI. International copyright secured.
All rights controlled by The Zondervan Music Group, Nashville.

Because

EDWARD TESCHEMACHER GUY d'HARDELOT

This arr. © 1987 by John T. Benson Publishing Company/ASCAP. International copyright secured. All rights controlled by The Zondervan Music Group, Nashville.

Eternal Life

ST. FRANCIS of ASSISI

OLIVE DUNGAN

© Copyright 1950 by The John Church Company. International Copyright Secured. All Rights Reserved. Used By Permission.

This Is Where the Candle Glows

Words by
DON KOCH and VINCE WILCOX

Music by DON KOCH

© Copyright 1986 by Paragon Music Corp./ASCAP. International copyright secured. All rights controlled by
The Zondervan Music Group, Nashville, TN 37228.

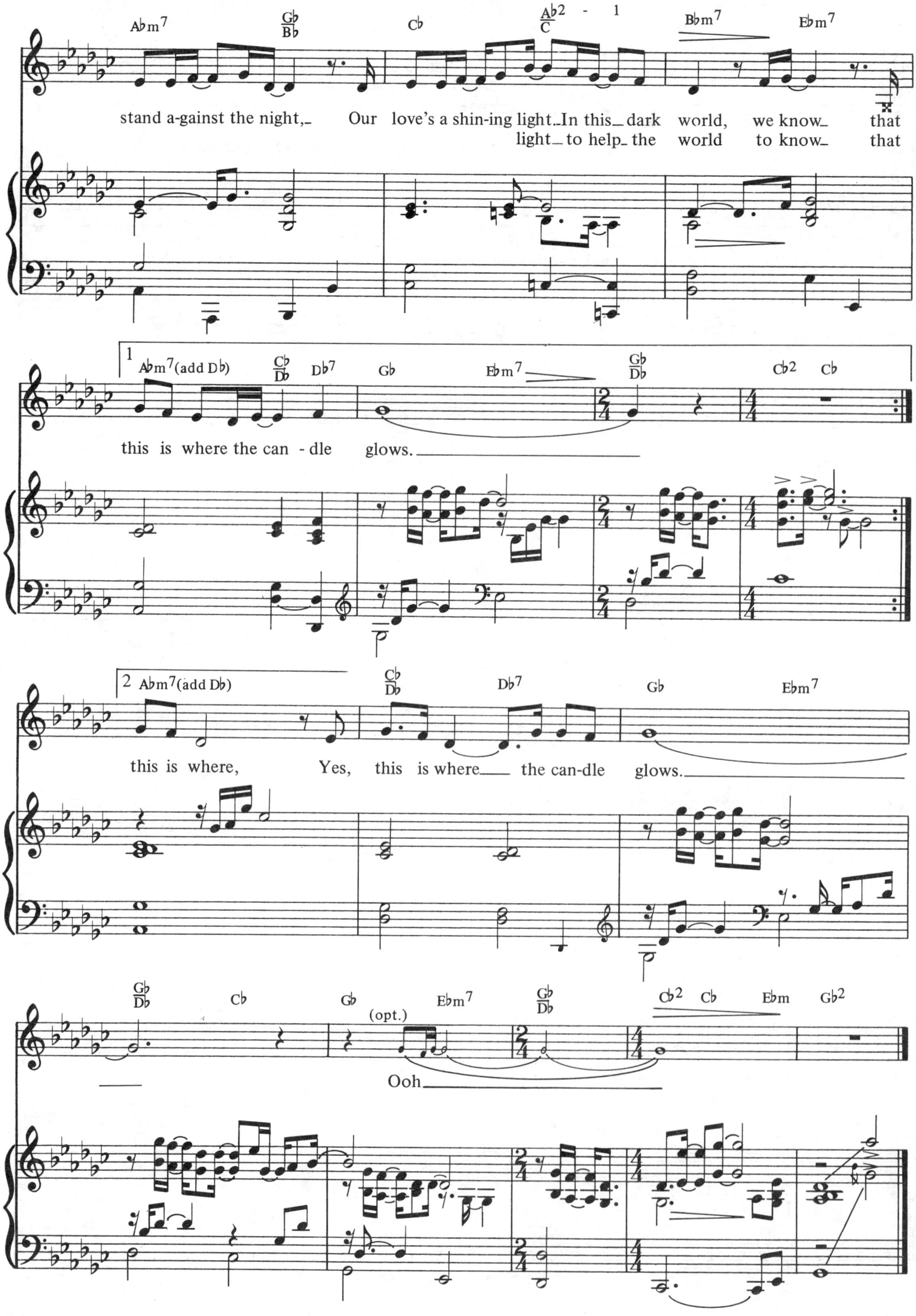
A♭m7 G♭/B♭ C♭ A♭2 - 1/C B♭m7 E♭m7
stand a-gainst the night,_ Our love's a shin-ing light._In this_ dark world, we know_ that
light_ to help_ the world to know_ that
1 A♭m7(add D♭) C♭/D♭ D♭7 G♭ E♭m7 G♭/D♭ C♭2 C♭
this is where the can - dle glows._
2 A♭m7(add D♭) C♭/D♭ D♭7 G♭ E♭m7
this is where, Yes, this is where_ the can-dle glows._
G♭/D♭ C♭ G♭ E♭m7 G♭/D♭ C♭2 C♭ E♭m G♭2
(opt.)
Ooh_

Morning Has Broken

ELEANOR FARJEON
Gaelic melody

Text reprinted by permission of Harold Ober Associates, Incorporated. © Copyright 1957 by Eleanor Farjeon.

Hearts of Joy
(A Wedding Invocation)

Words and Music by
GEORGE KING

We've asked you here to-geth-er in this place to show the world the things we've said in se-cret. Here I know it won't be out of place; hearts of joy re-leased, for all the world to see. Two roads meet, be-come as one;

© Copyright 1987 by Pleasant Hill Publishing/ASCAP. International copyright secured. All rights reserved. Used by permission.

Jesu, Joy of Man's Desiring

J. S. BACH

This arr. © 1987 by John T. Benson Publishing Company/ASCAP. International copyright secured. All rights controlled by The Zondervan Music Group, Nashville.

Household of Faith

© Copyright 1983 by StraightWay Music (ASCAP). All rights reserved. International copyright secured. Used by permission of Gaither Copyright Management.

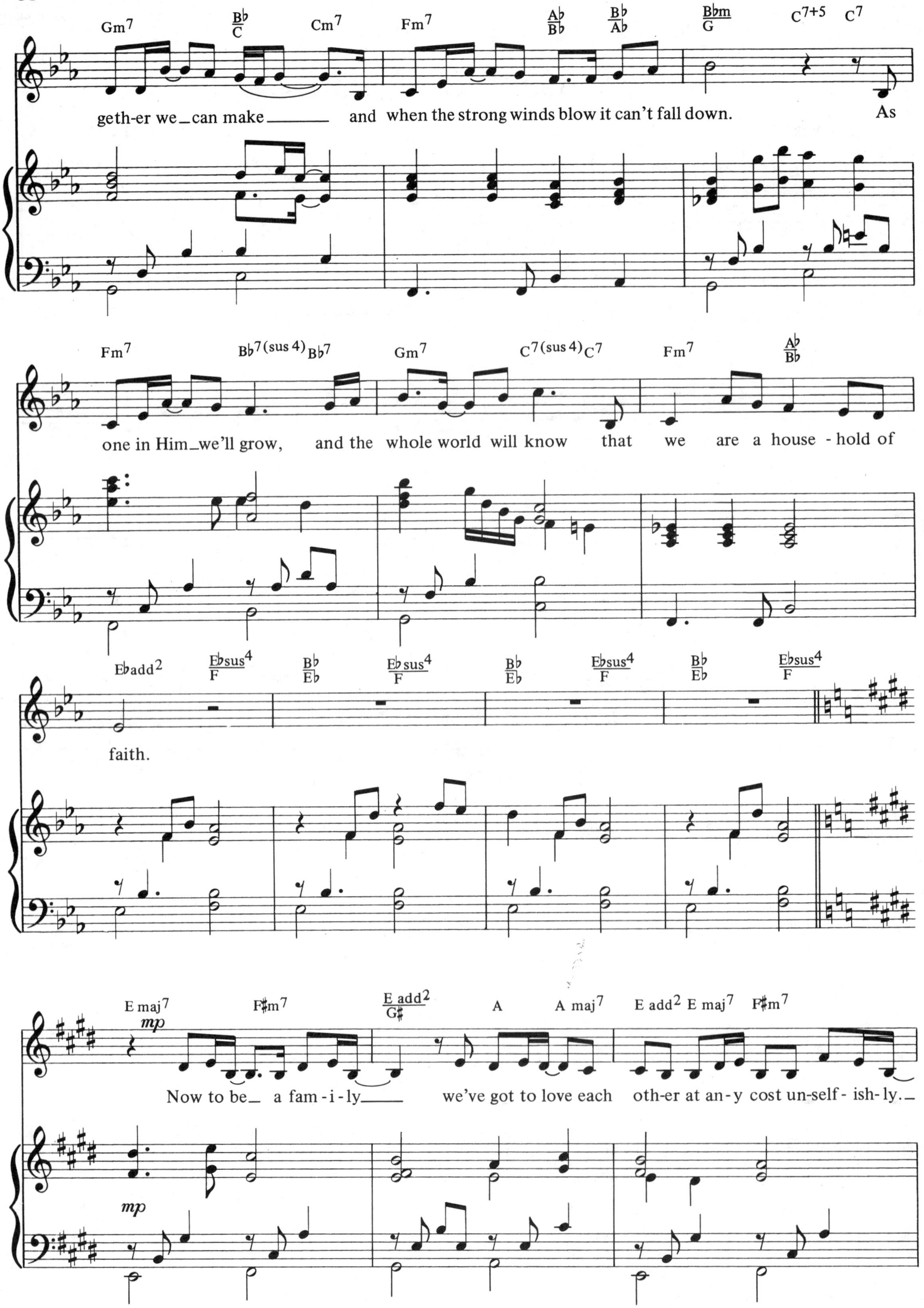
Gm7 Bb/C Cm7 Fm7 Ab/Bb Bb/Ab Bbm/G C7+5 C7
geth-er we can make and when the strong winds blow it can't fall down. As
Fm7 Bb7(sus 4) Bb7 Gm7 C7(sus 4) C7 Fm7 Ab/Bb
one in Him we'll grow, and the whole world will know that we are a house - hold of
Ebadd2 Ebsus4/F Bb/Eb Ebsus4/F Bb/Eb Ebsus4/F Bb/Eb Ebsus4/F
faith.
E maj7 F#m7 E add2/G# A A maj7 E add2 E maj7 F#m7
mp
Now to be a fam-i-ly we've got to love each oth-er at an-y cost un-self-ish-ly.
mp

Trumpet Voluntary

JEREMIAH CLARKE (1659-1707)

This arr. © 1987 by John T. Benson Publishing Company/ASCAP. International copyright secured. All rights controlled by The Zondervan Music Group, Nashville.

Only God Could Love You More

Words and Music by
DWIGHT LILES and NILES BOROP

© Copyright 1986 by Word Music (div. of Word, Inc.)/ASCAP and Bug and Bear Music/ASCAP. Bug and Bear Music exclusive adm. by CS Music Group, Inc., P. O. Box 202406, Dallas, TX 75220. International copyright secured. All rights reserved. Used by permission.

Wind Beneath My Wings

L. H. and J. S.

LARRY HENLEY and JEFF SILBAR

Smoothly, in a moderate tempo

It must have been cold there in my shad-ow

to nev-er have sun-shine on your face.

© Copyright 1982, 1983 by WARNER HOUSE OF MUSIC and WB GOLD MUSIC CORP. All rights reserved. Used by permission.

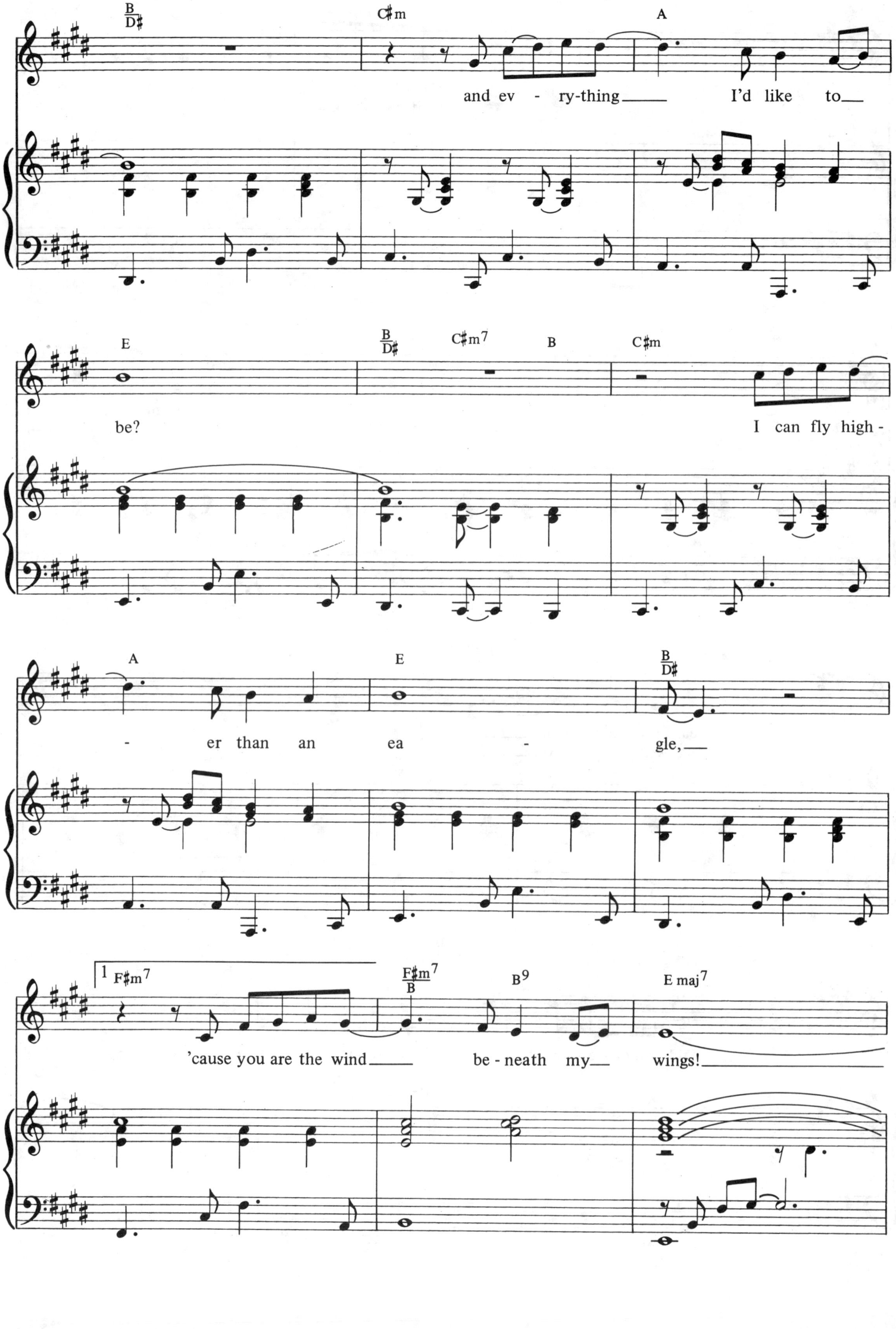
B/D♯ C♯m A
and ev - ry-thing I'd like to
E B/D♯ C♯m7 B C♯m
be? I can fly high -
A E B/D♯
- er than an ea - gle,
1 F♯m7 F♯m7/B B9 E maj7
'cause you are the wind be - neath my wings!

Make Us One

Words and Music by
DENISE and DWIGHT LILES

© Copyright 1986 by Paragon Music Corp./ASCAP and Bug and Bear Music/ASCAP. Bug and Bear Music exclusive adm. by LCS Music Group Inc., P. O. Box 202406, Dallas, TX 75220. International copyright secured. All rights reserved. Used by permission.

Entreat Me Not to Leave Thee

CHARLES GOUNOD

This arr. © 1987 by John T. Benson Publishing Company/ASCAP. International copyright secured. All rights controlled by The Zondervan Music Group, Nashville.

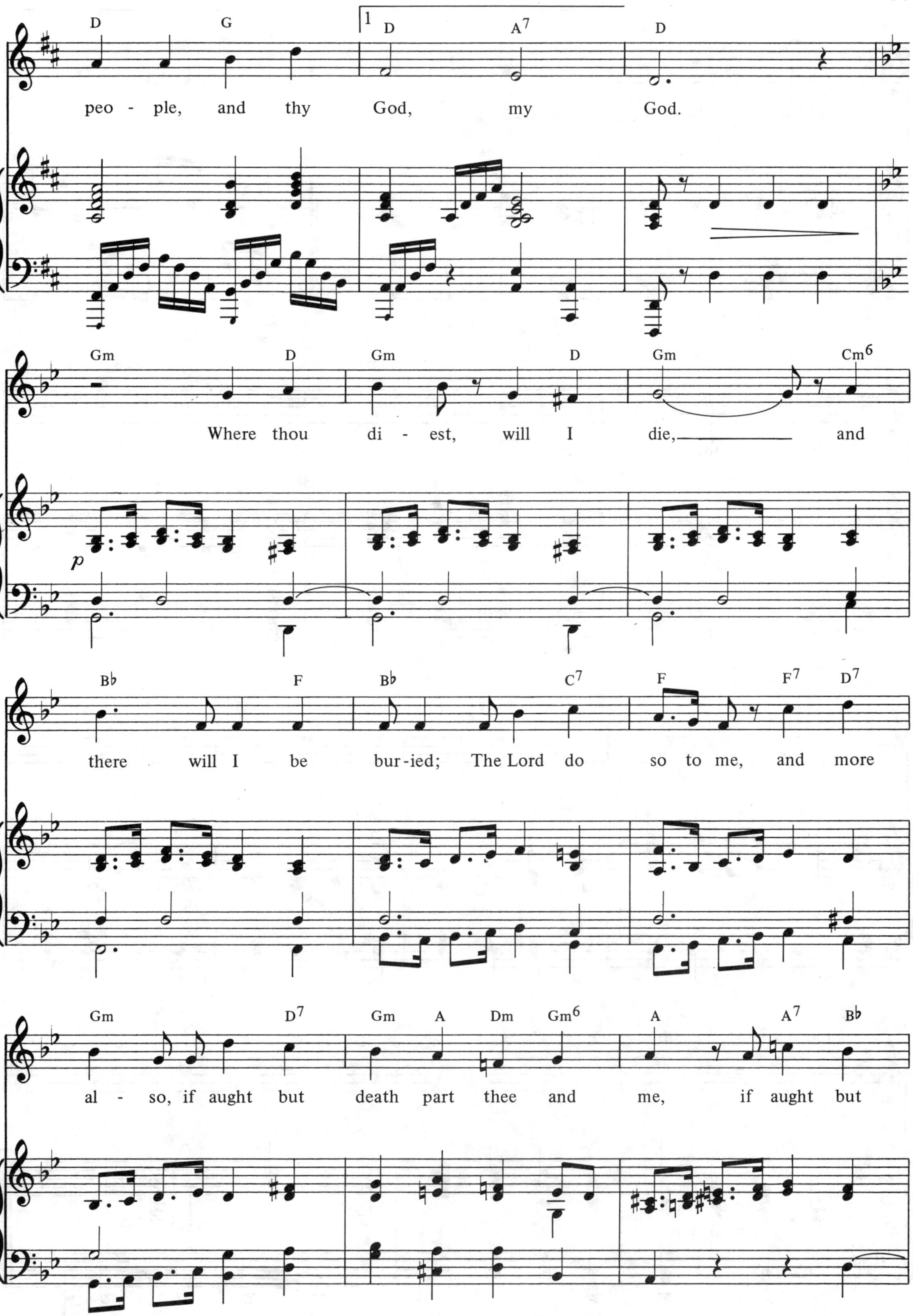
D G 1 D A7 D
peo - ple, and thy God, my God.
Gm D Gm D Gm Cm6
Where thou di - est, will I die, and
p
Bb F Bb C7 F F7 D7
there will I be bur-ied; The Lord do so to me, and more
Gm D7 Gm A Dm Gm6 A A7 Bb
al - so, if aught but death part thee and me, if aught but

Savior, Like a Shepherd Lead Us

Words attributed to DOROTHY A. THRUPP

W. B. BRADBURY

This arr. © 1987 by John T. Benson Publishing Company/ASCAP. International copyright secured. All rights controlled by The Zondervan Music Group, Nashville.

The Father Says, "I Do"

Words by BRENT LAMB, LAURIE LAMB and PAUL GUFFEY

Music by BRENT LAMB

© Copyright 1987 by Paragon Music Corp./ASCAP and Singspiration Music/ASCAP. International copyright secured.
All rights controlled by The Zondervan Music Group, Nashville.

Wedding March

FELIX MENDELSSOHN

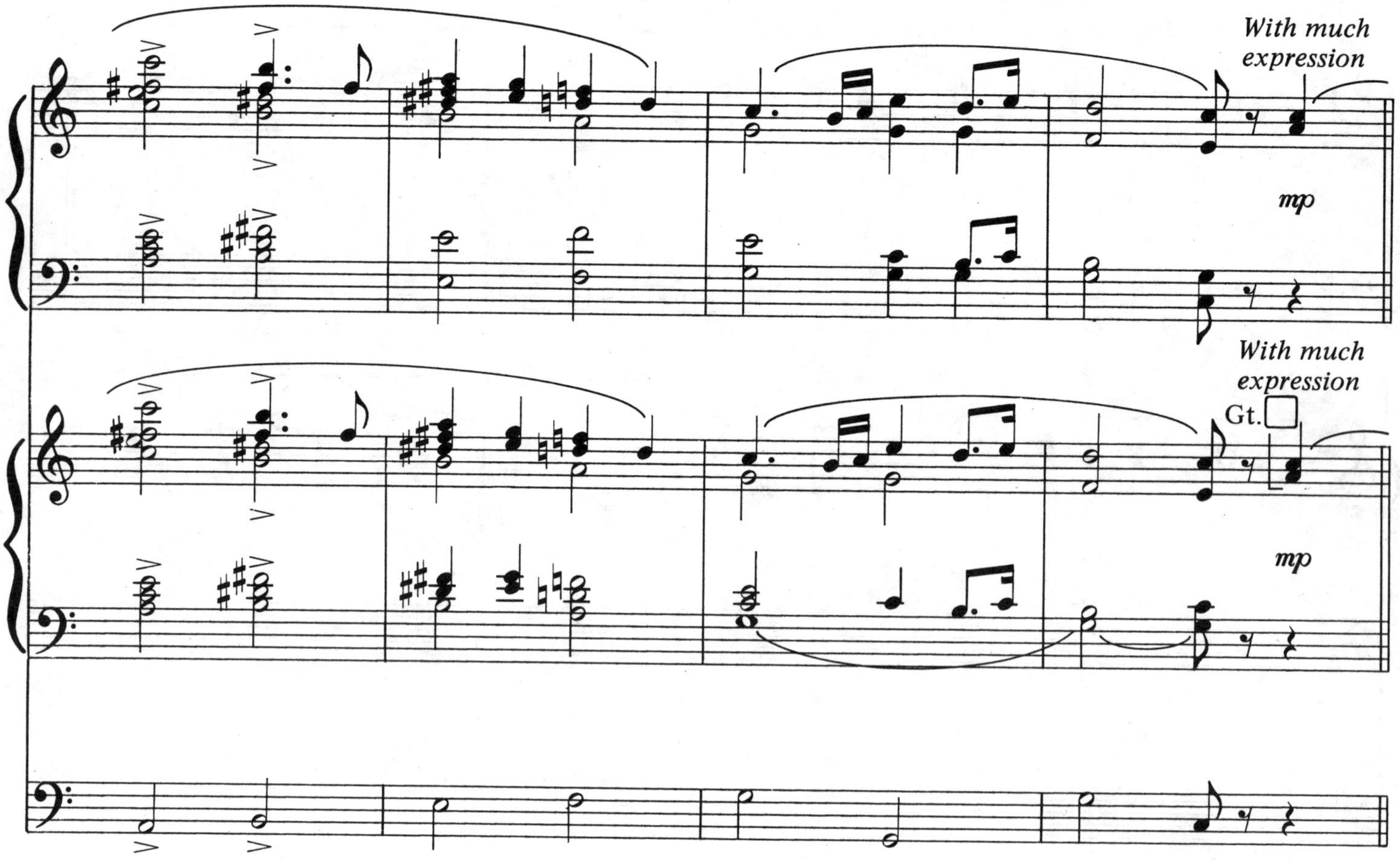
With much expression
mp
With much expression
Gt.
mp

r.h. legato
r.h. legato
Sw. G Reed 8' off

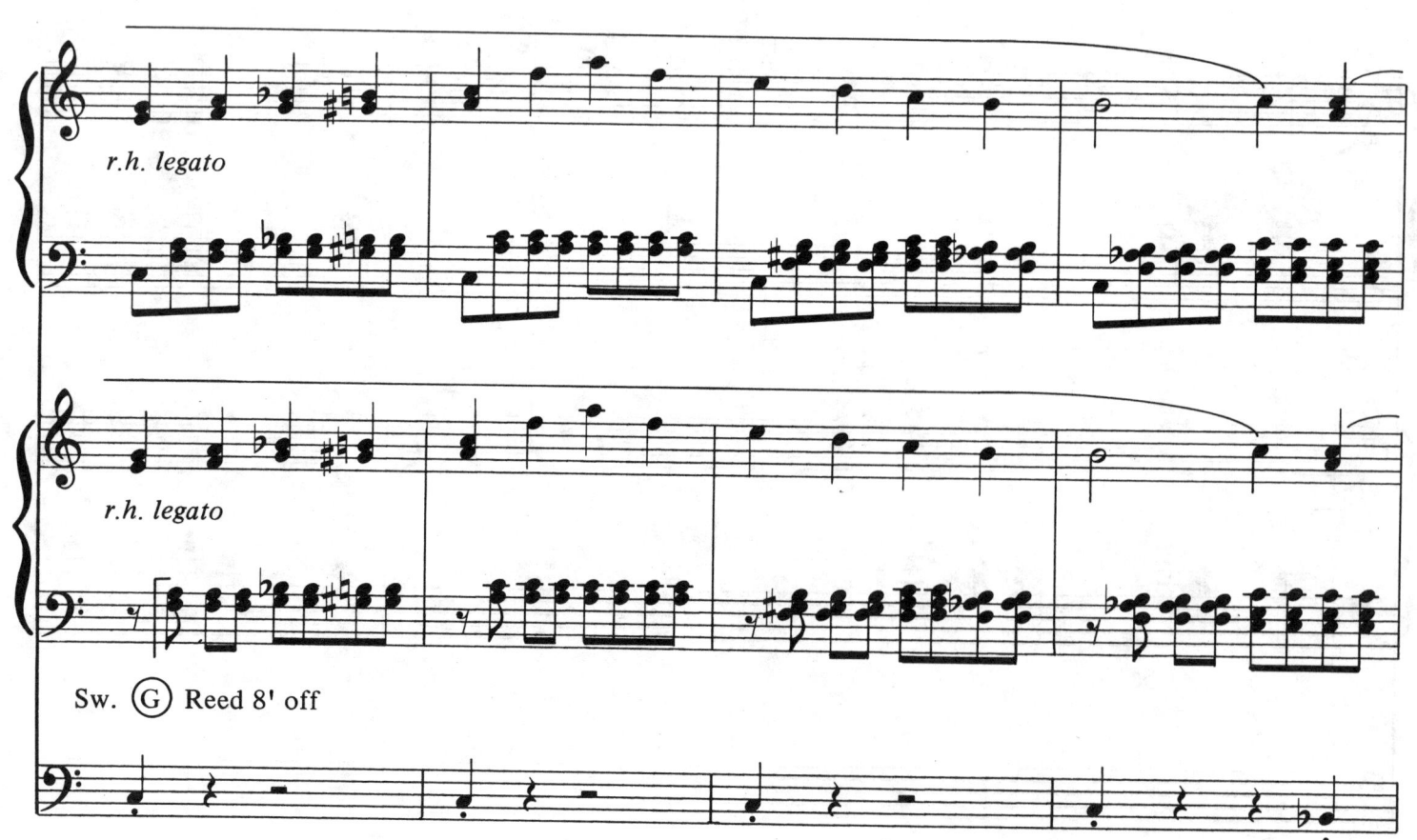

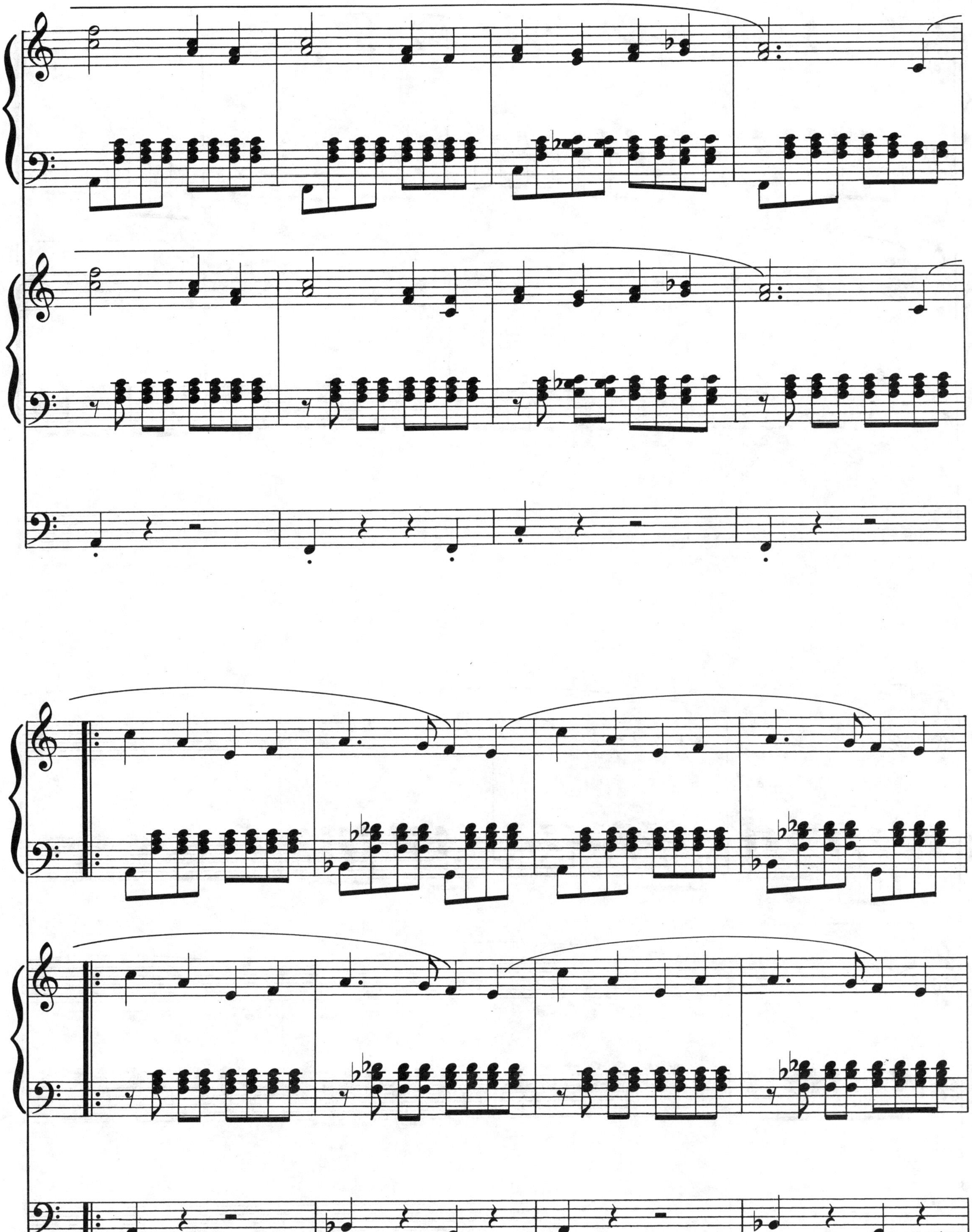

114

116

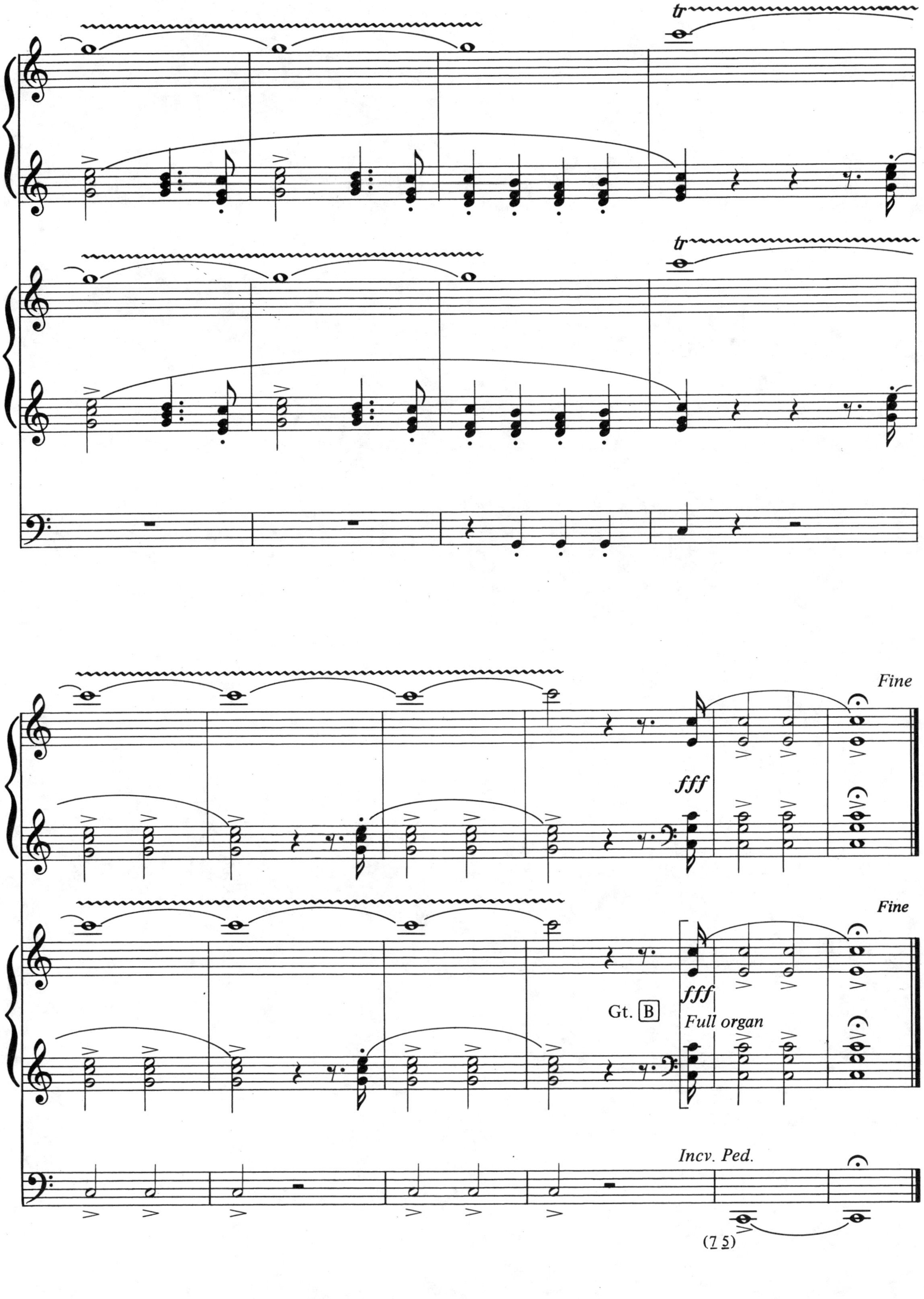
tr
tr
Fine
fff
Fine
Gt. B
fff
Full organ
Incv. Ped.